# Valley

## Story Keeper Series
## Book 20

Dave and Pat Sargent (*left*) are longtime residents of Prairie Grove, Arkansas. Dave, a fourth-generation dairy farmer, began writing in early December of 1990. Pat, a former teacher, began writing in the fourth grade. They enjoy the outdoors and have a real love for animals.

Sue Rogers (*right*) returned to her beloved Mississippi after retirement. She shared books with children for more than thirty years. These stories fulfill a dream of writing books—to continue the sharing.

# Valley Oak Acorns

Story Keeper Series
Book 20

## By Dave and Pat Sargent
and Sue Rogers

## Beyond "The End"
By Sue Rogers

Illustrated by Jane Lenoir

Ozark Publishing, Inc.
P.O. Box 228
Prairie Grove, AR 72753

Cataloging-in-Publication Data

Sargent, Dave, 1941–
   Valley oak acorns / by Dave and Pat Sargent
and Sue Rogers ; illustrated by Jane Lenoir. —
Prairie Grove, AR : Ozark Publishing, c2005.
   p. cm. (Story keeper series ; 20)

   "Be helpful"—Cover.
   SUMMARY: Everyone was bigger than
Mausi. She had to look up, and they had to
look down to talk to her. One day she found
a way to talk face-to-face to her big brother—to
be equal! It was very important.
   SBN: 1-56763-941-0 (hb)
        1-56763-942-9 (pbk)

   1. Indians of North America—Juvenile
fiction. 2. Maidu Indians—Juvenile fiction.
[1. Native Americans—United States—Fiction.
2. Maidu Indians—Fiction.] 1. Sargent, Pat,
1936– II. Rogers, Sue, 1933– III. Lenoir, Jane,
1950– ill. IV. Title. V. Series.
   PZ7.S243Va 2005
   [Fic]—dc21                     2003090098

Printed in the United States of America

# Inspired by

the calm, meditative canopy of a tree.

# Dedicated to

teachers who guide children to celebrate the things they do well and to tackle the things that take extra effort.

# Foreword

Everyone would soon be gathering large sweet Valley Oak acorns. The big granary by Mausi's house must be filled to the top so there will be enough acorns to make mush, soup, and bread all year. Women and children usually gather the acorns. Men and boys shake the trees. But this year, things will be different! Mausi and Nodin have a surprise!

# Contents

If you would like to have the authors of the Story Keepers Series visit your school, free of charge, just call us at 1-800-321-5671 or 1-800-960-3876.

# One

# Bountiful Harvest

"Never eat the meat of a bear, Mausi," said Mother. "A bear is just like a person. You might be eating your grandfather!"

"But Grandfather's soul has gone along the path of the sun to rest on Histum Yani (Spirit Mountain)," I said.

"That is right," she answered. "But now his spirit might be in the grizzly bear. Respect the power of the grizzly, Mausi. Use the hide as a robe on your bed, or make regalia for ceremonies from it. But remember to never eat bear meat," she cautioned.

"I will remember, Mother. And besides, the basket of yellow jacket larva that Nodin brought us this morning will taste much better. Will you cook the larva tonight, Mother?" I asked.

"Yes, my child," said Mother. "Now, bring me more fern roots for this basket."

Mother and my sisters were very busy making baskets. I was helping. We had many uses for baskets. We cradled babies, cooked and prepared food, stored supplies, carried loads, and caught fish in baskets. Baskets were also used as bowls, shallow trays, traps, hats, and seed beaters. The stitches in my mother's baskets were so fine they were hard to see.

"Mausi," called my oldest sister. "Please get more water from the river. These yucca leaves are too dry to weave."

It would soon be time to gather acorns from the tall oak trees. Acorns were our most important food. The Valley Oak acorns were the largest and sweetest.

We needed many baskets to gather enough acorns to feed our family. Mother's measure for how many acorns she needed was to fill the granary. Then there would be enough to make mush, soup, and bread all year for her family. It took six people gathering for two weeks to fill the granary.

Mother wove our granary and Father put it up. He put it on stilts near our house. It was as tall as

Father. An opening at the bottom let the acorns fall out when needed. I could barely reach it. The top was covered to keep the rain out. Squirrels and birds did not like that.

Before the acorns could be used, they had to be cracked, hulled, and cleaned. Then they were pounded into flour. Mother had a basket hopper she used for pounding acorns. It had an open circle in the bottom.

Mother placed the hopper on a grinding stone, filled it with acorns, and pounded away through the open circle with a rounded pestle.

Once the acorns had been ground, Mother spread the mixture in a shallow basket. She heated water and poured it over the mixture until all the bitter taste was gone.

Our village was built on a knoll along Feather River. We could see anyone coming long before they got to the first house. The first house was ours.

My brother, Nodin, kept watch on the river and valley below and on the path that led up to the village. He watched for intruders. His lookout was in a secret place.

Our winter house was big and round. The floor was three feet into the ground. A log and pole framework was covered with grass, brush, tules, and a heavy layer of earth. This made a nice warm house for cold winters.

The summer house was made of cut branches that were tied together and fastened to sapling posts. This was covered with brush and dirt. It faced the morning sun to miss the heat from the afternoon sun.

## Two

# Shady Characters

Work on the baskets was finished for the day.  I was hurrying down to Feather River, named for the feathers floating on the waters.  I often came here when I had time to be alone.  But today I had a special reason to be here.  Nodin had promised if I could find his secret lookout, I could visit him any time.

There were two things I knew. One, Nodin always went toward the river.  Two, his lookout had be in a tall tree for him to see everything. There was one thing Nodin did not know. He did not know that I had been climbing trees since my fourth winter. I had never talked about climbing trees because only boys climb trees—boys and me!

It all began one day when I saw a tree in the forest near our house. It had limbs that grew close to the ground. It had so many leaves that it looked like a bright green mountain. I felt a little like one of the cautious creatures in the forest as I drew near that big tree. My foot almost lifted itself onto a lower limb. I grabbed another limb with my hands and the next thing I knew I was sitting in a high crook of the tree! I could feel the spirit of the tree. Then and there, as the green tree swayed in the wind, my bond with trees was formed. I have climbed trees ever since.

When I reached the sandy strip beside the river, I lay flat on my back. I looked up into every tree.

You saw a tree from the top down when you climbed it. It looked different from when you saw it from the bottom up. You saw mostly leaves, a lot of limbs, a few critters, some nests, and maybe a bird or two. But I did not see Nodin.

I moved to a different spot and tried again to see the hideout. I got the same results. So once again I moved and failed to see Nodin.

Now what? I sat down in the warm sand and pulled an acorn cake from a pouch around my waist. It tasted real good. I ate it very slowly. Suddenly, Nodin was by my side.

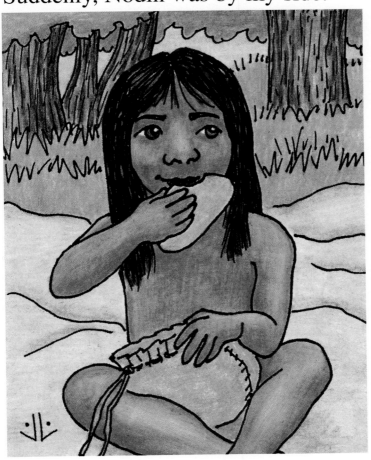

"Do you have another acorn cake Little Sister?" he asked.

"Sure," I said and smiled. "One for me and one for my brother."

As I handed him the acorn cake, I said, "I heard you slip on the limb of the tree just behind me. Your secret lookout is in it, Nodin!"

"I always knew you were a tricky one," laughed Nodin. He took a big bite of his acorn cake. "But tell me, Little Sister, how are you going to get to my lookout?"

"I will climb the tree, Brother," I said.

"It is very high," came Nodin's quick reply. "I am not sure if you can climb it."

We finished the cakes. Nodin said, "Come, Mausi. I will give you a lesson on climbing trees. One day soon you will be able to visit me in my lookout."

Nodin headed toward a small tree. I followed. Just before we got to the small tree, I ran ahead of Nodin and began to climb as fast as I could. I was in the top of the tree before Nodin even got to the trunk.

Nodin just stood there, looking up at me, too surprised to speak. Then he threw his head back and began to laugh.

"You are just full of surprises, Mausi," he said. "How long have you been climbing, Little Sister?"

"Since three winters, Nodin," I answered. "There is nothing I love more than climbing trees! Now, can we climb your tree?"

It was not an easy climb to the top of Nodin's tree. He was much taller, stronger, and faster than me. But I climbed all the way to the top.

It was so beautiful looking out from the top of that tree that it took my breath away. I could see forever. There the two of us sat, above, in, and beneath clouds of green—two "shady" characters!

Three

# A New Tree Shaker

I joined Nodin often in his airy perch. There I found peace and oneness with nature. There were birds and insects I had never seen on the ground.

"Is something bothering you, Little Sister?" Nodin asked one day. "You remind me of the creatures who use trees to escape their predators."

"I am not afraid that someone is out to harm me, Nodin," I said. "But—oh, Nodin—even if I told you, you could never understand. So I will say nothing."

"Let's see, Little Sister," said my brother. "We are high in the arms of a mighty tree, away from everything. Tell me what you are feeling."

For a while I sat, swaying with the tree as the wind whispered through its canopy. Finally I said, "When we are on the ground, you look down at me because you are so tall. Mother, Father, Grandmother, my sisters and brothers—everyone I know—looks down on me because I am smaller, Nodin. You even call me Little Sister. Until you let me climb your lookout tree, you did not know I could climb. No one thinks a little girl can do anything important.

"But climbing towards the sky, learning the tree's story in her bark and branches, I feel that I am equal with you and everyone else. The words began to rush now. "I can look down and see people on the ground. I am face-to-face with you, Nodin. Will you not call me Little Sister, Nodin? Will you not call me that anymore?" I cried.

Now it was Nodin's time to be silent. Finally he began to speak. "You are a wise one, Mausi. Perhaps you do not know why Father chose me to be the lookout for our village. I have trouble doing things that my brothers find easy. My hands will not move right to make an arrow point. Sometimes the arrows I make turn out flat," he said.

We both laughed at the thought of a flat arrow.

27

Nodin continued, "For some reason, Mausi, I see things backwards. I find it very hard to do some things. But I have always been good at climbing trees. Father told me that it is just as important to be able to protect our people from an enemy's surprise attack, as it is to shoot them with an arrow. I have always wondered if this is true. Thanks to you, my wise sister, you have made me know that it is. Yes, we are face-to-face in the tree. I am glad this makes you feel important. Now, I understand that it makes me feel equal too."

"Oh, Nodin," I said, "Besides protecting us, the music you make with your elderberry flute is the most beautiful music in the world. Why, none of the dances at our ceremonies would be complete without the rattle you made from deer toes. You are important to me, to our family, and to our tribe, Nodin!"

"All your help is important too, Mausi," said my brother. "I have counted the trips you make to the river for water. You keep fresh pine cones to brush our sisters' hair. I have watched you as you do your chores, then help others with theirs. Now, just wait until I introduce our newest and finest tree shaker at the acorn harvest this year. You won't be on the ground gathering acorns with the women this year. You will be in the tops of the trees, shaking the branches so the nuts will fall, my important sister."

"Thank you, Nodin," I cried. My arms flew around his neck.

It was time to climb down and
do my chores.

# Four

# Maidu Facts

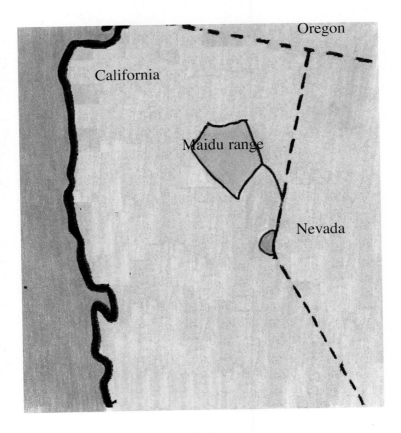

Maidu summer house, tule (bundles of water grasses)

This is a cutout view of an underground house.
Underground houses were used in winter.

32

These items are carried in the hands or worn in the hair. The squares are made of flicker feather shafts woven into small squares.

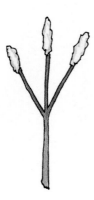

WAL-yet-teh
Trembler

Nisenan
Maidu hair plume

Konkow
Maidu motkin

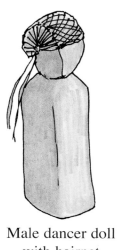

Male dancer doll
with hairnet

Maple bark doll

Maidu cradle

Cocoon rattle

34

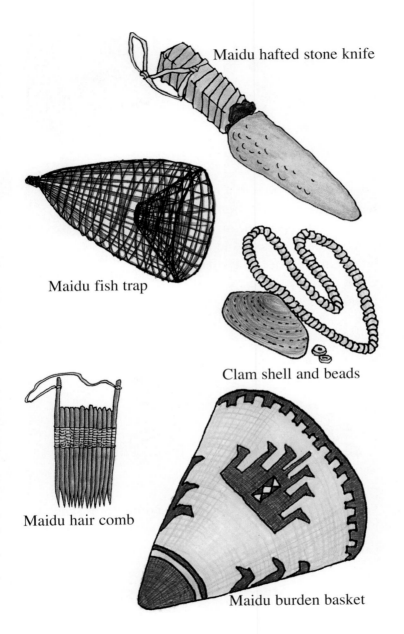

Maidu hafted stone knife

Maidu fish trap

Clam shell and beads

Maidu hair comb

Maidu burden basket

35

This is a large hole in a rock with straw in the bottom. Acorns are leached in the hole. The water takes out the bitter tannin taste. The small grind stones are called manos.

Valley Oaks are some of the tallest oak trees.

The community grinding rock outcropping

Valley Oak acorn and leaves

# Beyond "The End"

● Mausi used figurative language when she said that her people used baskets to "cradle babies" and when she spoke of Nodin and her sitting in the shade of leaves, calling them "two shady characters".

Words and images that appeal to the imagination and tell what things are like are figurative language. Words that tell what things actually are, are literal language.

Rewrite the last paragraph of Chapter 2, using literal language. Discuss the differences.

# *CURRICULUM CONNECTIONS*

● Mausi thinks climbing trees is a wonderful experience. You will understand if you have ever climbed one. There are rules and safety precautions you must learn and follow before attempting to climb a tree of any height. Learn how to take care of you and the tree. Read all about it at <www.treeclimbing.com/tci/tci-04.html>. Enjoy — but BE SAFE!

● If six people gather about 33,600 pounds of nuts in two weeks, how many pounds will each one gather? This will feed 16 people. How many pounds of acorns will each one eat?

● Some people use acorn meal today. Try one of the tasty treat recipes at <www.backwoodshome.com/articles2/clay79.html>.

● The acorn from the Valley Oak tree is a different shape from the acorns in my part of the country. Find a picture of the Valley Oak acorn. Compare it with acorns on the oak trees in your area.

● The Maidu used beads as a form of money. The beads were counted by tens and handled on strings. If a Maidu man wanted to sell a tanned deerskin, how many beads would he ask for it? How many beads would you expect to pay for a jug of salt?

● The Maidu believed that the eagle was a messenger to the Creator. What is another tribe that honored the eagle because they too believed that he carried messages above?

● Where do most of the Maidu people live today?

## THE ARTS

● Music is an important part of Maidu culture. Flutes of elderberry, pierced by a row of four holes, are played at a 45-degree angle and to one side of the mouth. Rattles made from about 30 deer toes, each attached to a separate buckskin thong and secured to a wooden handle, help set the rhythm for a dance. Clapper sticks are also rhythm instruments to accompany song and dance. They are made from a short length of soft wood. One end is split and the pith removed. Holding the unsplit end, you strike it against the palm. The hunting bow, with one end held in the mouth, is tapped or plucked. Of course, there is the drum. Make your own band and music for celebration.

## GATHERING INFORMATION

● A Maidu legend explains that the world is round and floats in a sea. It is held by four ropes. A shaking of these ropes makes earthquakes.

Why do you think there is a legend about earthquakes from the Maidu?

Look up the scientific explanation of earthquakes. Be sure to include information about quakes in or near your state. You might find the U.S. Geological Survey website of help at <www.earthquake.usgs.gov>. Make a report to your class.

TEACHER'S NOTE: There is valuable information about earthquake drills at website <www.csuniv.edu/Academics/Quake/EQ%20Drill.pdf> (It requires Adobe Acrobat.).

## THE BEST I CAN BE

● Do you know what Mausi meant when she said, "...learning the tree's story in her bark and branches?" There really is a story in a tree. The more you look at a tree, the more you will really see the tree — its space and location, its volume and structure, and its engineering and balance. You will see the uniqueness of each single tree. Every tree is different, just as every person's fingerprint is different. Learn all about trees. You can find help at <Nationalgeographic. com/kids>. Learn the value of trees. Learn how to protect trees. Today would be a good day to "HUG A TREE!"